Published by: Gabrielle Garcia

ISBN-10: 978-0-692-19526-0

Distributed by:

Gabrielle Garcia

Los Angeles, CA 90031

Printed and bound by Amazon CreateSpace

WHY YOU KEEP THINGS

GABRIELLE GARCIA

Special Thanks to:

Aby Ayala

Angel Valentin

Alana Parnaby

America Montes de Oca

Carly Blanchard

Cici Jevae Gordon

Cory Fong

Crystelle Reola

Dan Blachinsky

Eliseo Garcia

Gabriela Garcia

Gabriel Gutierrez

Giovanni Walker

Hannah Kuhar

Ivan Cortez

J.C. Herrerra

Jacqueline Grohs

Julian de la Rua

Joe Melgoza

John Mejia

Laura Gray

Lucy Shapiro

Michael A. Apodaca

Maria-Nicole Ikonomou

Marisol Medina

Michael Mott

Micah Perks

Miguel Sarabia

Nadia Karapetian

Sharon Sekhon

Sayo Fujioka

Tomas Benitez

Victor Robles

In Memory of Michelle Lozano

You will always be remembered

by your community

and your friends

We love you and will never forget you.

CHAPTER ONE

POESA

Reading poetry between the lines,
to understand the whole story.

Para Mi Mama:

I look at you and

wonder what childhood meant to

      you.

When I was a child,

you were always working.

I know you did it all,

              para tu familia.

I know que

          crisciste en el rancho.

Imagination spills from my mind and climbs into every-
thing I do.

Maybe it was a seed you planted,

so I could always tie the pieces I have of you back to-
gether.

Tortillas de maiz

                        pisos de tierra

                                       caballos y cabras.

You always talked about the lake beside your house

Where your mother washed pañales

and

blood red rags,

under armor.

Me imagino de tu niñez

observando el lago, el reflejo de tu cara.

Y nunca pensando en mi.

ALL IT TAKES

Reflections on windows and

A screeching halt on a train track.

                              Time melts my agitated mind

I skipped lunch,

to stare at the rims of a stranger's glasses.

And follow a speck of sunlight running along the
frames.

I meet this stranger's eyes—

Awkwardly smile.

Focus on the little kid sitting across from me, and his skateboard.

I follow its wheels, until I notice his mother staring at me.

Catch a scent of her way too heavy perfume, and look away.

Listen to the train. Let the rhythm seduce each limb.

Relax each muscle until fingertips fall onto the sides of my thighs.

Look past the window.

Don't think about her.

Don't think about her caramel skin.

Don't think about the way she was found.

Don't think about being 17.

Don't think about who did it.

Don't think about what it was like
back then;

You made it.

Right?

You don't have to think about
that anymore.

History, although lost at times—can never be erased. It is re-traced and re-lived by our memories and stories.

CHAPTER TWO

MUJER SABIA

Fátima was fifteen years old when she was kidnapped by the "love" of her life.

Most of the time, it was refreshing in Las Palmas, Durango, Mexico. Today however, was an unusually hot day. It was June, 1943 and Fátima sweeped the steps outside of her tía Rosario's adobe home. Her broom lifted dirt off the porch and into an alleyway. She gripped her wooden broom handle with so much force, her sweat left a slight mark. This was her new life, in her new home. She was taken in since Fátima's mother was too poor to afford shoes and other necessary expenses needed to raise a young lady. Rosario took pity on her. Here, she had food, clothes, work in the house and was surrounded by cousins. She was almost a lady. Almost.

Maybe it was love. Maybe it was something much more sinister. His name was Javier. He was tall, dark, and direct. His eyes pierced you like an arrowhead. He was extremely polite. Every time he passed by anyone he didn't already know, he would remove his sombrero and introduce himself; His smile came on cue afterwards, every time. It almost blinded his captives.

Javier was Fátima's older brother's close friend. To Fátima, he was just an older man. He fell in love with her the first time he laid eyes on her. He offered her an ultimatum in a tiny room at the back of the house, or so it's told. He asked her to come to the room with her, and that's when it happened. The proposition.

Perhaps Javier confessed he fell madly in love with her at that very moment, and grabbed her in his arms and explained he needed her by his side forever and ever. Or maybe, something else. She was given two choices: she could either choose to be with him, or stay in her new home. Not much was ever revealed to Fátima's first born daughter, or her daughter's daughter. Regardless, she chose a new life. And she grew to love it. Forever and ever.

She stood at 5' ft 3", and her smooth, dark skin shimmered on the lake she would inherit as Javier's bride.

Her entire life would revolve around her twenty one children; Except when the first four passed from complications. Pneumonia, sepsis, diarrhea, and pneumonia. These children would be forever remembered and never brought up again. The rest of her seventeen children would eventually discover what it meant to be part of the Sanchez family.

Anastasia was the first to survive. As a baby, she grew famous for a daunting and sharp stare. One day, Anastasia began vomiting uncontrollably. She was just a baby. Fátima feared the worst. No food, no water. Fátima was terrified her daughter would not survive, so she prayed. Javier on the other hand looked at his fifth born daughter and said only one phrase:

"Let God do what he will, we've spent too much money."

Two neighbors offered Fátima money so she could take her newborn to the doctor. These two neighbors were seldom remembered in the many recitations of the story. During the whole ordeal, she prayed to Santa Maria to let her daughter live. She was desperate. She made a promise—if her daughter survived, she would not cut her hair until she turned fifteen. Anastasia survived. And her hair was not cut until she turned fifteen.

Anastasia loved her mother. When she was four years old her parents were officially married by the church. Fátima wore a pink dress. She danced with her neighbors en la recepcion de boda. She looked beautiful. Her smile radiated so strongly anyone that looked her way instantly mirrored her expression. Anastasia clung to Fátima's leg and would cry if any man approached her mother. It was a beautiful ceremony, although the most simple in town. These were the stories Fatima told Anastasia as she grew older. She cherished them. Anastasia would sometimes misbehave, and her mother would spit out stories of her childhood as reprise. She would tell her daughter of the wound on her hand that never closed because it was always covered in dirt, and how she didn't have any food to eat, or shoes to wear, and here she was acting como una ingrata.

Anastasia would cry for hours—almost endlessly, not wanting to believe her mother lived such a life of hardship.

Then the guilt would come. Then, Anastasia would apologize and minimize her misbehaving. Once her brothers and sisters were born, Anastasia was bound to responsibility. She was the watchful sister of the sixteen Sanchez kids. She never got to be a child. She didn't mind. She loved her family.

JOE MELGOZA

CHAPTER THREE
FÁTIMA'S LEGACY

Anastasia sits on the edge of the lake as I wash our clothes. I have to sneak around so she doesn't follow me, pero ella me mira.

"No. Te. Muevas!," I tell her.

She gnaws on the gaeta que tiene and just stares at me. Pero sabe, she knows not to move otherwise she will fall into the lake and drown. I think she is staring at my bruises. I hope she can only see the ones on my arms. The ones on my arms are not as dark as the ones on my legs.

Anastasia sits on the edge of the lake as I wash our clothes. I have to sneak around so she doesn't follow me, pero ella me mira.

"No. Te. Muevas!," I tell her.

She gnaws on the gaeta que tiene and just stares at me. Pero sabe, she knows not to move otherwise she will fall into the lake and drown. I think she is staring at my bruises. I hope she can only see the ones on my arms. The ones on my arms are not as dark as the ones on my legs.

I use rags for her diapers, but they are covered in gusanos today. One by one they drop into the water. I wonder, if she'll ever remember this. The way she looks at me, with those eyes. My beautiful baby girl.

CHARLOTTE MOSS

CHAPTER FOUR
TRAUMA

Seven years later, Anastasia stands at 4'7 ft, weighing 85 lbs with light brown eyes and a posture straighter than the body of the shovel she uses to work. She looks at her mother one last time, before gently climbing into the lap of her tía Rosario. It will be the last time she will see her mother before moving to the city of Gomez Palacio, Durango.

She's headed for la cuidad.

Fátima wears a flowing white dress—a different personality to the brown and beige clothing she normally dresses in. Fátima does not smile as her first born daughter rides away. She is a stern woman. Anastasia watches her mother from the window of the truck.

Fatima notices her stare, the same look her little girl always held when she was thinking. It burned. Worse than the way petróleo burned her nostrils during dinner. She thinks about her children slipping away from her one by one, falling away from her like droplets in a pond. She wonders if this is her fate como mama.

Anastasia imagines the city to be a larger version of el rancho, where she was born along with seventeen other brothers and sisters. She knows it's her job to receive an education so she can get a job and help the family. She imagines la cuidad to have endless job opportunities.

Her stomach growls lightly. Each growl blasts off one after the other. She imagines the sound as if it were a group of screaming coyotes. When she was a little girl she once heard them far off in the distance, as if they were whispering about her. They were annoying things. But, she was good at drowning out noises, all kinds of noises throughout her childhood in fact.

She watches her tía open up a tortilla full of nopales. She licks her thin lips. The scent in her nostrils spreads quickly like a bomb, and reminds her of home. She thinks about the dinners she had with her family. The way they used to make fires to cook meat. She thought about the flames. There would be a fire in her father's eyes if he were to find out she's trying to learn how to read and write. She immediately shuts her eyes to put out the image. Once its gone, she can hear the sound of a train. She wishes it could take her somewhere even further away.

But she couldn't bear to be away from her family forever.

When she opens them, she realizes she lays in her one bedroom apartment in Lincoln Heights. She sits up from a daze, confused and clutching something.

CHAPTER FIVE
ANTES

Lincoln Heights, Los Angeles, 2009.

She looks at her wrists and stares into them for a moment. For what seems like the first time in 25 years, she notes the cracked skin. Her eyes slowly drift towards the picture frame in her hands, and she catches a reflection of her face in the glass. She squints, searching to see if the wrinkles are real.

She's clutching a photograph of herself at four years old. Her stare was so serious back then, she thinks to herself. She smiles. Lola, her daughter became fussy as a child when looking at this exact photograph. Lola always thought it was her, and cried if Anastasia told her the truth.

She was in the middle of re-arranging books, bags, and baby clothes in the giant CRT TV that served as a closet. It took up a quarter of their living room, and broke in 2003, but she still used the carcass of it to house various items. Even if they were broken or sticky, or old, she knew deep down inside they were items that she might one day use, or give to family in Mexico. Or maybe, one day when she had time she could sort through everything. Everyone else thought it was a piece of garbage. A useless trunk from the past. But to her, it was useful. It stored memories. She was saving everything for the day they moved out of their one bedroom apartment. Maybe one day she could go through it all. She had a couple carcasses around the house.

Her husband Rey and her daughter Lola always pestered her to throw it away. They never listened to her reasons, they didn't care. She had a lot of items and things like this TV. The old baby chair, the old toaster oven, the old microwave, the old sewing machine, the old telephones. Seven mattresses. Bags of clothes from the 80s. The piñata. Anastasia wondered if they would throw her away too, for looking old. For being outdated. They never appreciated her.

At times, she felt they teamed up just to attack. Just to make her feel ashamed. For what? For helping her family? For not having time to help herself? For keeping her memories locked up away in boxes? She wants to keep these things. Sometimes they break, but they will be used to fix other things, to rebuild them. Everything is useful. That's what she learned en el rancho. They would never understand. How could they?

She remembers placing all the heavy books at what used to be the bottom of the TV, but was now just a broken platform before drifting away on the couch. Her husband's university books detailing cosmologist astrology came first in the pile. She was very proud of Rey for graduating from a University.

Even though every book was covered in something sticky, she still remembers where she got each one, and who gifted them. Underneath a collection of dried out markers and glitter sticks, she found a pile of Dr. Seuss books she used to read to her daughter. She picked one up and set it aside.She dropped a pile of photographs, scattering them amongst stained clothes and sticky newspapers. Old baby and toddler clothes lay beneath a pack of never opened diapers from 1990.Anastasia heard Rey.

"Fucking goddamn it, tu's pinches gatos! Son of a bitch. This fucking house, the fucking cats pissed on my shoe! Mira!" Rey yelled.

Anastasia recoiled with pain. When she heard his voice, she pictured metal trays smashing on a concrete floor. She felt it something deep down in her throat. It wasn't just a sound, it was everything. It was guilt, shame, even physical pain. As Rey climbed over a pile of clothes, four cats jumped out from underneath the couch that sat just behind the front door. He sighed to notify Atanasia it's entirely her fault one or maybe a few of their five cats urinated on Rey's shoes.

She heard her dogs wake up from all the commotion. Five chihuahuas in the kitchen began to bark. She didn't have time to clean up their mess on the soaked newspapers laid out the night before. She shushes them. If Lola was here, she would tell Rey to "shut the fuck up." He listens to Lola for some reason. Maybe out of his guilt or shame, or shock that his little girl has no respect for him in these instances.

He used to be the type of man to complement Anastasia. The first time he laid eyes on her, she was wearing a yellow dress and taking adult school courses at the continuation school. They both continued their once-stopped studies in Mexico. They would receive their GEDs together. He asked her to marry him. Right then and there. She thought he was crazy. He sighed again. At 52 years old, Rey was tired. He was tired of supporting his wife. Not that he supported her financially, he supported her culturally, or so he believed.

Although Anastasia made the majority of the household income, Rey taught her things. How to drive stick, how to speak english, how to go to school. Few would understand, or even know, the reason Anastasia married Rey.

She still remembers the day she found out he was from Durango, Mexico. It was the day she gave him a chance. When Anastasia came to the United States at the age of 27, conocio Rey. He was a school bus driver. He knew how to get all over Los Angeles. He knew how to read maps. Anywhere she wanted to go, he knew how to get there. She remembers she thought he was strange, especially because of his first words to her— in front of monjas! Nuns she was talking to! She was actually quite disgusted. Que grosero. But, when she overheard someone mention he was from her hometown in Mexico, she couldn't believe it. Their childhoods in Gomez Palacio, Durango could not have been more opposite from one another. Rey grew up a city rat. Anastasia was a saint in the flesh.

He had no idea she was from his hometown. He just obsessed over her in the yellow dress. He called her every day for weeks. He knew there was something about her that was different. She seemed innocent, and kind. Not once was she quick to judge anyone or thing. It was as if her smile was permanently splattered across her face.

Rey was not machista, back then.

Anastasia was a live in caretaker for a family of three women. The eldest, named Maria grew weaker and weaker every day. Sometimes Anastasia needed help every time she bathed Maria or needed to change her diaper.

Rey was always there to help. Never once did he look away in disgust, or suggest she get a new job, like some men commented to Anastasia when she invited them over para cenar. Rey always brought cookies for the women when he came to visit, and Anastasia fell in love with his kindness.

Now, Rey sometimes jokes he never expected her to continue taking care of the elderly once they got married. But, she didn't mind. They were her family. It was in her blood. It was her gift.

CHAPTER SIX

AMERICAN DREAM

Today, it's different. Right now, she does not say a word. She picks up her nursing uniform and heads to work. She feels numb.

"Mañana, puedo limpiar la ropa, y los zapatos con Miss Mary," she thinks to herself. She closes her eyes and holds the expression for a long moment. Her face, long and delicate looks fragile. She feels helpless. Like an infant.

She tries to talk to her husband, but he calls her crazy, tells her she's dirty, and silences her. Sometimes she feels a wave of shame wash over her. She has stopped trying to talk to Rey.

Apart from taking care of the elderly at a nursing home, Anastasia works for an elderly woman near Hollywood. Her name is Miss Mary. Anastasia also takes care of Rey's mother, and the last of the three elderly women, Rosa.

She's been a caretaker her entire life.

The house Miss Mary owns is green and sits on a hill. The front porch, wide enough for twelve people to sit across, twinkles in the Southern California sunlight. Three steps lead up to the front door, adorned by two pillars. She feels like she works in a castle. She walks inside just as she does every weekend. She scrapes the bottom of her heels on the shaggy 60s carpet, blue on all edges and displaying a flower pattern in the center. The house smells like hidden cigarettes. The muffled scent hides like perfume waiting to be released from pockets of memory around each corridor.

Anastasia switches the TV off. Miss Mary left for her daily bingo, as she often did, since she had no children or grandchildren to care for, or check up on her. The dial clicks on the 1960s TV set. She walks towards the dining room and through the kitchen, out to the back. As she steps down the stairs she clutches her laundry bag close. Once done setting the clothes in the cellar to wash, she starts singing, badly. Anastasia feels happy pretending to live here, sometimes.

She throws her husband's shoes inside the lavadora. Her posture straightens. She lifts her chin and smiles. She does not have to walk through piles of things that have not been put away in Miss Mary's home. It feels like her home.

Maria-Nicole Ikonomou

CHAPTER SEVEN
DESPUES

Lola, 17, flips her hair. She leaves it there for a moment, waiting for the drip. She ain't addicted, she just got shit for free, so it was cool. Her boyfriend, Bryce, licks the left side of her neck gently. She laughs, and pushes him away.

They both reach for their skateboards, and run out the door, each racing for the pavement first. As they fall out of the doorway, giggling, Lola tiptoes around Bryce and jumps on her board. She kicks her back foot onto the floor as fast as she can, balancing her front foot in the top center of her blue skateboard. She skates down what seems like the biggest hill in the neighborhood. It's not. Avenue 31. It wasn't a hill at all really, but more of a slope. She had done it before, plenty of times. As Bryce catches up to her, his board carves closely to hers. It creates a shadow that swallows hers. A trail of nothing on the road, followed by something. Something dark, intangible. Something temporary.

The first time they kissed and the first time she ate shit on Ave. 31 are almost the same memory. Both times, she saw stars. Both served as a constant reminder that everything can change in an instant. Both made her feel invincible and fragile all the same. It should be noted Bryce's presence always caused a surge of adrenaline. Every time they kissed— her mind shattered. It was like an ice cube that hadn't frozen completely solid, breaking open and spilling. Crack, spill, rush-wave.

Her board wriggled and wobbled. The speed wobbles.

She flies off landing on her left knee and wrist. The asphalt on Ave. 31 said hello to her face. And she said hello back.

"Fuuuuuck!" she says.

"Godfuckingdamnit!"

"Ah shit babe, you alright? Let me go get you some ice from Burger King," Bryce says.

He power slides smoothly, to a controlled stop.

"Hold on, I'll be right back."

He twitches as he touches her.

As she sits on the curb waiting for Bryce to come back with ice, her phone rings. Three letters light up the screen— MOM. She rolls her eyes, and then, smiles quickly, battling with herself on whether or not she's happy to hear from her mom at this precise moment. She ignores the call. Her mother calls again. She puts her phone on silent.

She pulls out her baggy and sifts her pinky nail inside of it. She rubs it on her gums.

Joe Melcoza

CHAPTER EIGHT
AHORRA

Anastasia struggles to remember if she gave her tía her diabetes shot today.

She races to grab a paper towel as she sees a roach scurry towards the plato de carne she just made. She catches it. Suddenly she sees three baby roaches on the floor, and she quickly stomps each one out.

She looks through the fridge, passed bags of old pan, passed In N Out containers full of week old burgers and fries, passed a Filario's pizza box her daughter left four nights prior, and looks for her tía's insulin. There are bags and bags of food that act more as decoration, the collection of smells results in a scent you would find in a hospital trash can. She continues sifting for the insulin. She finds it underneath a half bitten apple. She slowly walks over and injects la tía Conchita.

In somewhat of a daze, she notices that she forgot remove the plastic cap on the pen. She closes her eyes in a tired familiar fashion. She walks towards the fridge and tries to find another pen, but spends ten minutes smelling different containers she can't remember what are for, or even contain. The smell of burned toast wraps around her shoulders and kisses her lips. She finds the pen. She walks slowly over. She injects the skin, puts pressure on the pen, and places a cotton ball over the area. The smell comes back; it starts to burn her nostrils.

She forgot about the toast. Now burnt.
Smoke spills into the room. She waves her hands franti-
cally to dissipate the smoke, but it's an endless cascade.
She cannot believe the amount of smoke coming from
that pinché toaster.

"Mom, what happen?" a young Lola asks.
Anastasia, startled, looks down. A seven year old Lola
giggles.

"Ma, donde esta mi pan?"
Lola laughs at her mom's terrified expression. La chiq-
uita hugs her leg.

"Mija!" Anastasia yells.
She grabs her daughter, she holds her hand and
says,   "Mija, mija, mijita."

She hugs her daughter, tightly. She closes her
eyes again, as tears stream down her face. She opens her
eyes and Lola is gone.

She runs to the restroom and splashes water on
her face. Suddenly the room looks like it was that same
day. Older, a little cluttered, maybe a bit disorganized.
A cockroach catches the gleam of her eye and she
stomps on it.
She wants to call her daughter but knows she
will not answer. Lola's always unreachable, and never
wants to speak with her mother these days.

46

CHAPTER NINE

SUNNY AFTERNOON

Lola is a particular type of person. She was slow to open up, and yet always ready to jump a fence and skate an empty lot. She had a fire inside of her. She was trying to prove herself to everyone and was always prepared to argue. She wasn't violent, just vocal. She wasn't tough either. She just thought she knew what it meant to be a girl from Lincoln Heights, Los Angeles.

Lola skates to her favorite hangout spot, the block. A row of small colorful houses along a sloped street lined with palm trees. The demographic of the area was pre dominantly Latino and Asian families. The smell of rice and beans roamed the area. What makes the block truly special though, is that six of her friends lived on it. The street Lola grew up on only had one other kid her age and he never came out of his house, so she loved skating to the block and being surrounded by her friends, who all seemed to be more or less equally apathetic about the world around them. She learned how to be cool here. They taught her how to jump fences, roll joints, look for sketchy people. She was one of them.

On the way there, the combination of smells sway her into a dizziness. She skates past a gas station. She smells diesel. She skates past a garbage can, she's unfazed. The scent of frijoles wafting past the corn peddlers however, makes her mouth water. There was a taco stand inside an alleyway she cut through to get to her friends. It always made her hungry, but since she didn't have any cash, she settles. She figures she'll stop at the shitty liquor store and swipe a bag of chips. She notices the store clerk, Claudia is busy watching her novella again. So she instead swipes a blunt wrap from behind the counter while Claudia does not pay attention.

She waits for her friends as they trickle away from the supervision of their parents and travel outside, one by one. Melissa was the first outside, and she offers Lola a session. Lola hands her what little weed she had and a blunt wrap.

Lola watches as Melissa finishes rolling up the blunt.

"Man, I used to love grape flavor, and ever since we burned it now I don't like it. We smoke that flavor like everyday," Melissa says.

"My bad, I swiped it from Claudia," Lola says. "Can you even roll Lola?"

"No. But I can break it up really good."

Lola sits on the step right underneath Melissa as they wait for their friend Jorge to come out of his house. "It's all good Lola, how you been? What'sup with you?" Melissa asks.

"Just trippin' cause my mom is being all strict and shit. She acts like I'm a kid," Lola says.

"Foo, all moms are like that," Melissa laughs.

"Well fuck, maybe I don't want to be a kid," Lola says.

"What's up with you, how come I never see you at school anymore?" Lola asks.

"Cause you never kick it with me. I'm there, sometimes, I'm tryin' to get that edumacation' too." Melissa says.

A smile sprawls across her beautiful brown face. The two girls stare at each other. Lola looks at Melissa and admires her. She looks like a real woman, her curves, her hair. She was beautiful, with caramel skin, and lips like an angel. She looks so tough. Melissa pokes Lola's stomach and hands her the blunt.

Jorge busts out of his house and screams at the girls.

"What's good bitches!" Jorge says.

"Let me get some of that," He asks, reaching for the blunt.

The girls roll their eyes, and start to talk about plans for the night. They talk about the carwash they had for the homie who passed away a few weeks back. They talk about who's on lockdown, and who fucked who.

Lola knew of a backyard house show and Melissa knew about a party, and they talked about where to hold the next session. The neighbors were starting to get bitchy, so they thought about the abandoned house. It must have been the warmest day in March. They feel the sun touch their skin, and bask in the freedom. No responsibilities. Except, the priorities of chillin'.

JOE MELGOZA

CHAPTER TEN

GIG

The scene was slightly different from the year before, but the booze brands were exactly the same. Before, there were thrashers and black metal shirts galore. Today, it was bandana's, khakis, mohawks, bob marley shirts and doc martens.

Everyone was standing around the pit trying to push whoever they could in. Fake studs flew into the sky, and were quickly swallowed by the cloud of dust from kicking feet. was The crowd was fucked up, or close to it.

It was a backyard in East LA on a Wednesday night, and it was known to everyone as 'The Gig'. At the door a big, tall, bald guy with tattoos on the back of his neck collected $3 for entry. Someone wearing a patched up denim jacket was trying to barter a beer for an 'x' from a purple Sharpie on the back of his hand.

Sometimes they drew dicks instead.
Not today.

"Wassup foo, lemme get a hit." Said the
Bald Door Man.
"Nah dick, this is my last one, I'll let you hit
the piece though." Said a long-haired, leather jacket
wearing kid named Gilbert.

Gilbert held out his tiny pipe filled with shit-
ty brown weed and handed it over. There was too
much reverb. The drums drowned out low growls
on the mic every singer put a little too close to their
mouth.
Moshing throughout the crowd is a little girl with
bleach blonde hair and doc marten boots. She
doesn't give a fuck that there are guys twice her size
in there. It's Lola's friend Dez. She always drank
Malibu and wore Testament shirts. Lola watches as
the music allows for a release of aggression only ap-
propriate for backyard shows.

A quick panorama of the dirt filled yard
reveals a group of kids snorting coke in the far left
corner. In another corner, someone passes a piece
to the left of the circle. All throughout the crowd,
there is a rhythm in the lifting of 32 oz and 40 oz in
the air and back at waist level. There's a cholito in
the back, spitting game to a girl who must have been
about fourteen.

"Ay, wassup', you're a rocker chick huh? Ay, if you want you can rock deeze nuts, mijita."

"Fuck you little boy," she says, flipping him off.

"Damn foo, she burned you! Chale, ey you're lil' boy from the hood now?" His friend says.
"Shut up dick…"
As the girl walks away, the two men stare at her. Their eyes, full of something violent follow her. She feels the stare on the back of her neck and walks slower, to spite them. She wasn't afraid, but she wasn't going to babysit them either.

The pit grows more intense with each drum kick. A short kid, about 5'6 flies into a man wearing a Raiders jersey. A fight ensues. Raiders jersey grabs a baseball bat casually behind a broken kid's chair, stuffed and forgotten in the corner. Someone throws a bottle. It smashes on the floor.

"HEY WHAT THE FUCK!?"
Everyone pauses.
"Who threw that? That's fucked up man." said Raider's jersey guy.

Within minutes, the cops arrive. Everyone chugs their beer. Spiky hair, bandanas, mohawks, doc martens, all single file out the back door. Raiders guy makes eye contact with the big tall man at the door. They nod.

"Happy birthday to you! Happy birthday to you!"

"Everyone! Happy birthday dear…grandma…happy birthday to you!" The crowd sings.

That's usually how they got out of tickets, it wasn't a big show, just a family party! East LA was full of those! You can't ticket everyone. The name part was always wrong, but whoever was the loudest set the answer up for everyone else.

Dez and Lola stayed behind. They're here for the abuela party. They go inside the house. That was the luck they held as the few women at these kinds of parties. Lola and Dez pack into the garage toilet, and look at their eyeliner.

"Hey you want a bump? Jesse gave it to me for free, so it's cool," said Dez.

"Yeah fuck it, thanks," said Lola.

She walked into the living room. Astounding. Although the party was full of men, somehow, all the people who were allowed to stay were the women. She watched as all, mostly underage girls laughed and enjoyed the free Mickeys and Modelos. She looked at Dez. They both rolled their eyes, but stayed anyway. It was an uncomfortable truth. One she was not ready to face.

J.C. Herrera

Maria-Nicole Ikonomou

CHAPTER ELEVEN
REBEL

A forty oz sits on the table, with condensation dripping down as fast as Lola's hips thrusting into someone else's. She doesn't really know what she's doing, but she likes it. She feels mature.

The red hot ember from a skinny joint fades in and out, slowly until it turns off. Bryce could never roll joints. Her malt liquor sways gently back and forth, humming to the rhythm of the bed. It's Tuesday, and she ditched the theater class her mother enrolled her in.

Lola was satisfied, for a moment. She didn't need to get free shit today since she found her adrenaline in the arousal of Bryce. She loves him, but she feels like he is so nice, almost too nice. Lola doesn't know why he loves her back. She falls asleep, for an hour, and awakes to the sound of Bryce's absence. Her neck was cold. She always felt his breath on the side of her neck while they napped.

She finds him in the kitchen making a sandwich in his pristine four bedroom apartment, one that didn't have any bed bugs, roaches, one on the other side of town.

"Do you want some?" said Bryce.

"Yeah I'm down, make me that mother-fucking sandwich."

Bryce's mother is at work late tonight, and his grandmother lays in her room soundly asleep. Lola doesn't feel guilty about having sex while Bryce's grandmother was home. She knew that she couldn't hear them, since Bryce's home had five rooms and a very long hallway. The distance between rooms made it seem like they weren't even home together.

Lola smacks her lips, as she flicks the nail polish off her thumb.

She sits across from Bryce as she watches him

eat. She watches his light blonde hair as it falls in front of his eyes. Just as she is getting up to go hug his skinny waist, her phone rings.

The name "RUDY" lights up her screen.

"Thiiiss bitch," said Lola, with a smirk splattered across her face.

"Hey."

"They found a body," he says.

"Holy shit, what? No way! Where?" she asks.

"They think it's Melissa," He says.

"What?—" She says.

In a matter of milliseconds, Lola's ears rumble as she clenches her earbuds. while She scrunches her forehead in confusion. She grinds her jaw.

The world around her gets loud, and dark, her vision fades and comes in, she's inside of a Jazz rendition. She's in a nightmare.Lola jumps up and then quickly sits down again. Tears stream down her face. Bryce looks at her with a worried look. He doesn't say anything. He sits there waiting for her to end her conversation. He's been yelled at before for being too concerned about her lifestyle choices.

"Who told you?" She asks.

"I just saw her like two nights ago. What the fuck," She says.

"Michael told me. Don't tell anyone yet. Her family is looking for her. We are hoping it's not her," Rudy says.

CHAPTER TWELVE
SAINT

Anastasia had just finished her shift at the nursing home. She walked down Baldwin st. The bottom of her feet dragged along the pavement. Her arms were crossed. She looked down as she walked, and with each step her feet became heavier. She hadn't seen Rey in two days since she worked the swing shift. She hadn't seen her daughter for three days either. Lola had been staying the night with Bryce and going straight to school.

Anastasia thought about Las Palmas. The way the sun kissed burned the top of her head when she sat outside. It wasn't bothersome at all, in fact she loved the heat. How good her clothes smelled when she air dried them near the lake. There was never really any other smell quite like it. She thought about her cousins and her abuela. The way her father's horses bowed their heads each time they grazed on heno. She missed home.

She didn't have a home in Los Angeles. It wasn't the same. She just worked, and worked. And for what? Her family didn't love her. No one cared about her. Not Rey, not Lola, not her job, not Miss Mary, not her tia. She had nothing.

She walked past the woman who stood outside in the sun selling chips and soda.

"Hi Anastasia, como estas? Que bonito tu pelo!" she says.

" Hola, Mireya." Anastasia smiles.Anastasia saw a rubber band on the floor. She bent down to pick it up.

"Oh I can use this to roll up all the newspapers in the cocina." She thought to herself.

As she was bending down to pick up the rubber band, a man collecting cans and bottles stopped her.

"Señora, porfavor go inside your home. There's a killer on the loose."

"Que? What are you talking about?"

Mireya overhears this and pushes her cart over.

"No, es verdad Anastasia, una muchacha de 17 años. They found her, on the side of the road."

Chapter Thirteen

Aftermath

Two weeks after Rudy's phone call Lola comes home at midnight. She was out drinking at the park. She was with a boy notorious for always being on the street. His parents, drug addicts and always out as well. She thought he was cute. She felt like she could learn from him. There was something about his nose. She definitely felt adrenaline around him, even more so than with Bryce. She knew it was wrong, but she couldn't help it. Who cared what she did? It's not like it mattered.

She enters the apartment and tries to go straight to her room, but is interrupted on the way there. Her parents were fighting. Again. As she walks into the house the smell of cat piss hits her face the same way shame does when she remembers she had sex that night. She was ashamed in front of her parents, she felt like she let them down. She didn't feel powerful anymore, not when looking at her parents as they fought in their one bedroom apartment. Not when she knew their entire family did not have anywhere to go when they wanted to be alone.

"Los pinches gatos orinaron en mi ropa Atanasia!" Her father yells.

Her mother had been crying. She holds her tongue as she watches Lola step inside the house. She ignores the smell of marijuana with all her might, and looks at her daughter's face.

"Mija, como estas?" Anastasia asks.

"Bien." She says.

Her dad looks at her with love, and for the first time in a long time, a concerned compassion. It's as if they are friends in this moment. His brown face naturally softens as he speaks. Maybe he was happy she was home, maybe he was just glad to take his anger and attention off Anastasia.

Lola had a great relationship with her dad, it was the way that he treated her mom that made her upset and lose respect for him. She hated the way he seemed to ignore her, or forget her. She always wondered if her mom was smarter than her dad. Maybe she just needed to learn Spanish more to connect with her mom. She couldn't speak it well enough to have conversations with her mother the same way she spoke to her dad. Lola knew that when her mother spoke Spanish she sounded so intelligent and poetic. She was ashamed she forgot how to speak the very language that *was* her.

Her mom forces her to sit in her lap. Her father watches and then quickly looks down at the wooden floor, he sees a few roaches in scurry away. Lola slowly walks over. Carefully, so as not to push the wind around her into them. She knew she smelled like malt liquor and weed. Maybe if she walked very slow, they wouldn't smell it.

She is looking down, but there are tears welling up in her eyes. She looks up. Nope, too late. She begins to cry. All at once, she remembers her friend Melissa, the shame, the shit she got for free, lying all the time, and not believing in her mother. She thinks about having sex, she thinks about her adrenaline each time she does a line, she thinks about her one bedroom apartment, with bed bugs and roaches and cat piss. She thinks about her parents and how she just wants them to be happy. Why wasn't she happy?

Her breaths start to get heavier and heavier, quivering with each inhalation, and she begins to shake.

"Mija, calmate." Her mother pleads.

Rey and Anastasia grab Lola and guide her to the couch, the cats jump off the cushions and watch her cry. Her parents, now on each side of her wait for her to speak. Her mom starts to comb her hair with her fingers. Lola flinches, but doesn't move away. Rey sits with his back hunched over and his head in his hands. He sighs. They sit there with her, waiting patiently for her to speak. Lola can't. They all sit there patiently for her to say something.

"I can't believe it." Lola says.

"Ya se mija." Anastasia says.

They sit in silence for a few minutes.

Her mom tries to think of something, anything so that she could wipe this face of adulthood off her little girl's face. She remembers, a very special gift she was preparing for her daughter. She hesitated.

"Mija, te quiero enseñar algo."

Anastasia pulls out a Dr. Seuss book from the TV. It was the book titled, "Oh the Places You'll Go!"

Lola smiles, she's upset, and confused. Her vulnerability quivers in delight, it is a moment her childhood is allowed to peek through her face.

"Why?" Lola asks.

"Open it." Anastasia says.

Lola opens the book, and sees that her mother wrote her a letter on the first page, it's dated from ten years ago. She skims it and turns the page —this one was from nine years ago, another letter —eight years ago, and another, she flips through each page and realizes her mother wrote on each one in Spanish on each day of her birthday for her. Lola starts to cry even more.

"Porque lloras mija?" Anastasia asks.

"Because my friend is gone. Because mom, every year I will get older, she will stay the same age. Because I can't believe it." Lola says.

"I know Lola." Rey says, wiping tears from her face, his eyes gleaming with tears.   "She went to your elementary school, do you remember that?" Rey asks, unknowingly missing the point.

"Yes Dad, I know." Lola says. "I'm sorry Mija," her dad says.

"If I knew who did it you know, I would kill the sonofabitch," he says, with an accent. "Ven," he tells her. "Have you been drinking?" He asks, smelling her breath. "No mija, acuérdate que paso a tu tía. You know, you get me so angry when you drink," he says.

"I wasn't drinking, someone spilled it on me," she says.

She raised her eyebrows. She thought he always kept his thoughts to himself. Lola grabs the Dr. Seuss book. She begins to read the first page.

"Siempre acuérdate que tu mama te quiere. Te quiero mucho-mucho-mucho mija. Yo quiero ser tu amiga y tu mama. Siempre te puedo ayudar, eres mi rayito de sol. I love you always."

Her mind slows down. She looks at her mother and lets go of her clenched fists. The tears on her face drip slowly across the frame of her nose. Her face falls forward. Her hair, now stuck to the side of her face is protecting her from her mother's loving eyes. Lola glances at the lonely teardrop sitting on the tip of her nose. She laughs.

She thinks about Melissa. She thinks about her bright blue top the last time she saw her. She thinks about that day there was a carwash being held for her friend's older brother who passed away, and how Melissa and Lola were the only two holding up signs for the car wash the entire day. Anastasia looks at her and kisses her forehead.

"Mija, te acuérdas cuando estabas chiquita?"

Lola's breath slows down. She touches her Dr. Seuss book, and smiles.

"Si," She says.

Lola stares at Anastasia. She notices her wrinkles. She notices the small whisker on the side of her cheek. She notices the way her left eye is slightly puffier than the right. She wants to tell her so many things. She's sorry, she's sorry for doing drugs, she's sorry she can't understand how her mom feels. She's sorry she doesn't speak better Spanish. She's sorry she doesn't have a big house, for her things. She's sorry. And ashamed.

Lola looks at her mother, and in an instant all the shame and guilt morphs into something she cannot explain, something that came deep from within her, like a gift. She feels pride. She lets her mother caress her hair.

In this moment, she is seven years old again.

Chapter Fourteen

Espejo

It's difficult to look in the mirror

And ignore

parts of me that are you

Tu eres
Yo soy

Tengo mucho miedo

de ser audaz

Pero nunca voy a olvidar

Maria-Nicole Ikonomou

CHAPTER FIFTEEN

THE BLOCK

Lola skates to the block. It's quiet. She's the first one there. Slowly, people trickle out of their homes. Her friends, Brian, Victor, Eric, Isaac, Dez and Rudy sit on their bikes and skateboards. Everyone's quiet. "What's up then," Rudy asks everyone.

"Your face, ass." Dez says.

"My face is not an ass, ass." Rudy says.

"Shut up, everyone knows what's up. We're all fucking sad, can we just talk about it?" Says Lola.

"Why you have to get all fucking emo Lola, no one wants to talk about it. It happened. It's fucked up. I don't want to talk about it OK," says Brian.

"I want to talk about it." says Dez.

"Look it's fucked up. We all saw her at the beginning of this month. She was here. And now, she's not. Who fucking did it? How's her mom feel? That shit makes me sad, you guys won't even let me walk home."

"We all know it's fucked up Dez! That's why we're going to the funeral. No one is going to forget about it. I've already fucking cried, OK. I'm done with that shit right now. Can someone just lend me a light?" says Brian.

He lights his cigarette and sees Lola pulling out a small baggy.

"Lola what the fuck are you doing? Are you fucking stupid? Your friend just died and you're out here killing yourself slowly?"

"Maybe."

"You know he's just trying to fuck you right? What about Mr. perfect Bryce? What you're too hood for him? Get out of here." Brian says.

Rudy walks up to Lola and smiles. He grabs the bag, crumbles it, and throws it down the sewer hole.

"Don't be doing that no more ok." He smiles.

Lola laughs. She's nervous. All her friends begin to stare at her.

"I thought you were better than that Lola. What would your mom think? Shit, your parents are cool. Why you out here trying to act like you've got it bad?" Brian says.

Lola looks down. Her cheeks are red. She tries to skate away, even momentarily to get out of the hot seat, but her friends block her. It's not really an intervention, just a confrontation to stop being such an idiot. She rolls her eyes. She pulls out her phone. She smiles.

"Is it that homeless kid?" Rudy asks.

"No."

"Yes."

Rudy grabs the phone. He tells the person on the other side to fuck off. He hands Lola back her phone, while maintaining the strongest eye contact he's ever given her. Everyone looks at Lola. She feels her face burn with embarrassment, but maintains eye contact. She smiles.

"Pass me the blunt then," she says.

Brian passes her the blunt. He sucks his two front teeth.

Rudy gets close to Lola's face.

"Hey." he says. "Are you sure you want to do this?"

"Yeah dude," she says, exhaling.

She puts her head on his chest and closes her eyes. She was seventeen.

She could smoke weed. Right? It wasn't that other stuff, so it was cool. She felt embarrassed. She let some tears out, and Dez came closer and hugged both Rudy and Lola. Everyone was silent, but in that moment something changed. Their bodies were full of something warm. Something big. Everyone felt it in the circle.

Maybe one day, Lola would move away. Maybe she would mature. Or maybe, she would stay in this town forever with her friends. Drinking 40 oz. on the block, going to local shows, and being someone for her family. Something did change inside her in that moment.

Lola didn't know what she wanted. But, she knew she was glad to be alive. She was alive, and Melissa wasn't. So she had to make it count. For her. For her mom.